MY NOAH'S ARK

MY NOAH'S ARK

Story and Pictures by M. B. GOFFSTEIN

Harper & Row, Publishers

New York | Hagerstown | San Francisco | London

Library of Congress Cataloging in Publication Data
Goffstein, M. B.
My Noah's ark.

Summary: An old woman fondly remembers a lifetime
of experiences related to a carved representation of
Noah's ark she has had since childhood.
[1. Noah's ark—Fiction] I. Title.
PZ7.G5573Mz   [E]   77-25666
ISBN 0-06-022022-8
ISBN 0-06-022023-6 lib. bdg.

To my niece,

Sarah Goffstein

When I was a little girl,
ninety years ago,

my father made me an ark.

And I know he had fun
building it,

because once I heard his voice
behind a closed door,
booming like God's:

"Make it three hundred cubits long."

The Noah he carved
had a hammer in one hand
and a mop in the other,

and Mrs. Noah carried a saw.

Two spotted leopards,
two meek sheep,

two gray horses,
and two white doves

were already in their compartments

in the ark,

when my father gave it to me.

The smaller gray horse looked sad,
and I always stroked her
with my finger,

until to this day

there is not much paint left on her,

except for her two little eyes,
which look grateful.

Over the years, as I grew up,
my father added more animals:

a pair of brown bears,
a bull and a cow,

a hen and a rooster,
two striped tigers—

and oh, I enjoyed playing with them!

When I got married,
my husband teased me.

But I remember how gently
he carried the ark
to my new home.

I taught our children
the story of Noah,

and how their grandfather shouted
behind a closed door:

"Make it three hundred cubits long."

Now everyone is gone,
and the ark holds their memories.

Our fun and sorrow
seem to form a rainbow,

and it warms me
like sunshine.